Down in the Jungle

retold by
Mandy Ross

illustrated by
Elisa Squillace

Child's Play (International) Ltd
Swindon   Auburn ME   Sydney
© 2005 Child's Play (International) Ltd   Printed in China
ISBN 978-1-904550-32-7
7 9 10 8 6
www.childs-play.com

Down in the jungle
Where nobody goes,
There's a great big crocodile
Washing his clothes.
With a rub-a-dub here,
And a rub-a-dub there,
That's the way
He washes his clothes.

Tiddly-i-ti,
Boogie-woogie-woogie!
Tiddly-i-ti,
Boogie-woogie-woogie!
Tiddly-i-ti,
Boogie-woogie-woogie!
That's the way
He washes his clothes!

rub-a-dub
rub-a-dub

Down in the jungle
Where nobody sees,
There's a huge, hairy monkey
Scratching his fleas.
With a scritch-scratch here,
And a scritch-scratch there,
That's the way
He scratches his fleas.

Tiddly-i-ti,
Boogie-woogie-woogie!
Tiddly-i-ti,
Boogie-woogie-woogie!
Tiddly-i-ti,
Boogie-woogie-woogie!
That's the way
He scratches his fleas!

scritch-scratch
scritch-scratch

Flippety-flap
Flippety-flap

Down in the jungle
Where nobody hears,
There's a fine young elephant
Cleaning her ears.
With a flippety-flap here,
And a flippety-flap there,
That's the way
She's cleaning her ears.

Tiddly-i-ti,
Boogie-woogie-woogie!
Tiddly-i-ti,
Boogie-woogie-woogie!
Tiddly-i-ti,
Boogie-woogie-woogie!
That's the way
She's cleaning her ears!

Down in the jungle
When nobody's there,
There's a big daddy lion
Combing his hair.
With a comb-over here,
And a comb-over there,
That's the way
He's combing his hair.

Tiddly-i-ti,
Boogie-woogie-woogie!
Tiddly-i-ti,
Boogie-woogie-woogie!
Tiddly-i-ti,
Boogie-woogie-woogie!
That's the way
He's combing his hair!

comb-over
comb-over

Down in the jungle,
It's a bit of a shock,
There's a young lady rhino
A-twirling her frock.
With a twirl-around here,
And a twirl-around there,
That's the way
She's twirling her frock.

Tiddly-i-ti,
Boogie-woogie-woogie!
Tiddly-i-ti,
Boogie-woogie-woogie!
Tiddly-i-ti,
Boogie-woogie-woogie!
That's the way
She's twirling her frock!

twirl-around
twirl-around

twinkle-toes
twinkle-toes

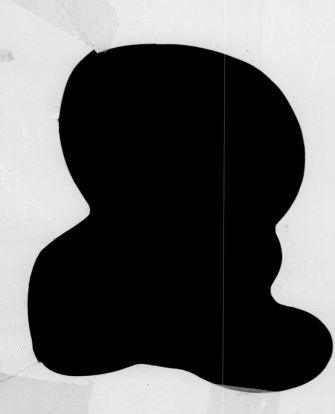

Down in the jungle
I just caught a glance,
Of a pretty purple parrot
Learning to dance.
With a twinkle-toes here,
And a twinkle-toes there,
That's the way
He was learning to dance.

Tiddly-i-ti,
Boogie-woogie-woogie!
Tiddly-i-ti,
Boogie-woogie-woogie!
Tiddly-i-ti,
Boogie-woogie-woogie!
That's the way
He was learning to dance!

Down in the jungle,
It made me turn pale,
I saw a long slinky snake
Who was wiggling his tail.
With a wiggle-wiggle here,
And a wiggle-wiggle there,
That's the way
He was wiggling his tail.

Tiddly-i-ti,
Boogie-woogie-woogie!
Tiddly-i-ti,
Boogie-woogie-woogie!
Tiddly-i-ti,
Boogie-woogie-woogie!
That's the way
He was wiggling his tail!

Down in the jungle
When the stars are bright,
I saw the jungle animals
Dancing all night.
With a boogie-woogie here,
And a boogie-woogie there,
That's the way
They're dancing all night.

Tiddly-i-ti,
Boogie-woogie-woogie!
Tiddly-i-ti,
Boogie-woogie-woogie!
Tiddly-i-ti,
Boogie-woogie-woogie!
That's the way
They're dancing all night!